CAREERING CREATURES

WHEN THE ANIMALS WENT TO WORK!

✉ carolynalmay@hotmail.com

ISBN: 978-1-5272-0014-2

Text editor

Clare Phillips

Illustrations

Laura Liberatore ©

Graphic design

Clementina Cortés

Carolyn May • Illustrations Laura Liberatore

Careering Creatures

When the Animals Went to Work!

With thanks to my wonderful parents

CONTENTS

The Referee

We never will forget, of course,
A most enthusiastic horse.
Frenetic Freddie was his name –
A brave ambition brought him fame!
As from the outset, as a foal,
He had an all-consuming goal.
He dreamt, he yearned, he longed to be
A famous football referee!
He watched the TV in the yard
Outside his stables really hard,

And when there was a soccer match,
He'd crane his head outside the hatch,
Devouring every single kick.
It really was what made him tick!
He knew the stars and where they played,
He knew how much they all got paid,
He knew that shoot-outs could be cruel,
He even knew the off-side rule!
He couldn't play himself, he knew –
He had four legs instead of two;
But referees, they did advise,
Could come in any shape or size.
So Freddie followed up his dream
And wrote off to the England team.
He lay awake at night and willed
His greatest wish might be fulfilled,
But weeks went by. He hid away.
It all looked bad, until one day
A letter came – he opened it.
It said, "Dear Freddie, if you're fit,
And good at blowing whistles hard,
And giving out the odd red card,
We need a ref the first of May."
(Why, that was just two months away!)
He sank, delighted, to his knees
And wrote back straightaway, "Yes please!"
Our Freddie knew this *was* his break!
He gave up eating chocolate cake

And threw his body into training –
Never mind if it were raining!
He raced around the huge arena,
Getting fit and slightly leaner.
He practised gruelling training drills
And galloped up the steepest hills.
The other horses thought he'd flipped.
"He's had too many oats!" they quipped.
But after weeks of torture, Freddie
Knew at last that he was ready!

Another letter did arrive.
It said, "The match will start at five.
We thought we'd tell you in advance
That England will be playing France,
And so the famous Marcel Zeem
Will line up in the Frenchmen's team."
Our Fred could not believe his eyes –
He felt like he had won a prize.
He knew of Marcel Zeem's endeavour
To be the greatest player ever.
(Furthermore, he had good reason –
He'd scored ninety goals this season!)
So Freddie packed and took the train.
He gazed out through the windowpane
And suddenly felt slightly scared –
Suppose he wasn't quite prepared?
But then excitement took fear's place
And Freddie grinned his happy face.
He bought a sandwich – shrimp with eggs –
And settled back to rest his legs.

Within an hour, Freddie stood
With heroes of his childhood –
From Chelsea, Spurs and Man United.
Freddie was just so excited!
And all the stars were really nice.
To Freddie it was paradise.
Until one player, Marcel Zeem,
Came up and shattered Freddie's dream.
"A horse?" he said unpleasantly.
"In France we eat your meat for tea.
A steak on legs and on our pitch!"
He laughed so hard he got a stitch.
Embarrassed, Freddie turned away.
He didn't know quite what to say.
But then a small girl in a scarf
Came up to get his autograph,
And Freddie felt a glow of fame.
He couldn't wait to start the game!
The trumpets blew, the ball appeared,
Whilst eighty thousand fans all cheered.

It should have cast a magic spell,
But Freddie didn't feel so well.
He had a sudden tummy ache –
His knees began to slightly shake,
And everything felt hot and limp.
Perhaps he'd had a dodgy shrimp?
Now Freddie had an awful fear
That he might soon have diarrhoea!
Unfortunately, it was too late
To go back through the entry gate.
The players lined up in position
Whilst Freddie had a different mission –
To cross his legs and keep it in.
But no – the match, it must begin!

So Freddie blew his whistle twice –
The teams were off within a trice!
The England Captain, Alan Yield,
First kicked the ball way up mid-field.
But then the French team sent it back
And soon began their own attack,
Whilst Freddie bravely stayed the pace,
Though with a grimace on his face.
The ball was passed to Marcel Zeem,
Who neatly dodged the England team
And sprinted straight towards the goal,
With most impressive ball control.
Just one defender could impede
The French team from a one-nil lead!

Marcel was faster than a train;
He charged up like a hurricane!
But then he did a dreadful foul…
The poor defender gave a howl
As Marcel's boot tore up his shin
And tripped him over on his chin!
The England team were all aghast
And Freddie blew his whistle fast.
The football stopped, the crowds all booed,
But Marcel Zeem was very rude.
"You stupid horse – don't stop ze game
Because zis nincompoop is lame!"
The poor defender clutched his knee
And rolled around in agony.
He looked so very woebegone,
They quickly brought a stretcher on.
"Red card!" yelled someone in the crowd,
And Freddie's heart beat very loud.
Could he send off, all on his own,
The greatest player ever known?
"Red card!" the chant began to rise,
And Freddie, fearful, shut his eyes.
There came the voice of Alan Yield,
"I think this man should leave the field."
So Freddie blinked and swallowed hard,
Then scrabbled for his small red card.
He raised it with a trembling hoof,
And Marcel nearly hit the roof!

He screamed, "Now look, you piece of meat,
You beat yourself a quick retreat,
Or otherwise, I swear, I'll make
You into tasty bits of steak!"
"It was a foul," poor Freddie wailed.
This plea for mercy duly failed.
Marcel whipped out a carving knife
And Freddie galloped for his life!
He tore across the pitch in terror,
Knowing he could make no error.
The Frenchman followed with a cry,
The savage knife raised near the sky!
His eyes were wild and nostrils flared.
The cameras rolled and fans just stared.
Then something awful came to pass.
As Freddie charged across the grass,

His dreadful tummy re-emerged
And something inside strongly surged.
He couldn't stop it coming out;
His bottom formed a waterspout
And squirted a *disgusting* poop.
It looked a lot like chocolate soup!
Worst of all, it kept on coming,
Flooding out from Freddie's plumbing,
So soon there lay in Freddie's wake
A brown and quite revolting lake!
Poor Freddie was just mortified.
There wasn't anywhere to hide.
At least his stomach felt more pure
Without this river of manure.

Meanwhile, the madman Marcel Zeem
Ran up and with a mighty scream,
He threw himself at Freddie's tail,
But Freddie flinched and watched him sail
Head-first towards the diarrhoea –
There came an overwhelming cheer,
As Marcel landed with a splat
And looked just like a sewer rat!
The dung was plastered everywhere –
Across his mouth and in his hair.
The Frenchman made a total scene.
He kicked and screamed – it looked obscene!
And Freddie watched with great dismay
As Marcel Zeem was led away.

Respect for Marcel dropped to zero,
But meanwhile Freddie was a hero!
The phones were ringing within hours,
"We need this horse to grow our flowers!"
So Freddie has hung up his boots
And now, instead, he contributes
To horticulture - Chief Adviser
At 'Freddie's Famous Fertiliser'!

The Detective

In England lives a dog called Rose,
Who has the most tremendous nose.
If you have fish for tea today,
She'll smell it twenty miles away.
If you don't bathe, although you think
Your Mum won't know, to Rose you stink!
And if you never wash your face,
Just wipe it on the pillowcase,
One sniff around your cheeks and lips,
And Rose will smell those tea-time chips.
The wax collected in your ears,
The pea that's been in there for years,
The bogeys hanging from your nose;
They all smell terrible to Rose!

* * *

Now even as a pup, Rose knew
Exactly what she had to do:
That with her sense of smell so strong,
Her passion for what's right and wrong,
Rose knew she would be most effective
Working as a dog detective,
And using her amazing snout
To sniff those thieves and robbers out!

Rose studied, trained and worked so hard,
She earned a place at Scotland Yard,
The famous London centrepiece,
Headquarters of the Met police.
But, to her rather great surprise,
For months she did not once lay eyes
On nasty criminals or cases,
Let alone exciting chases.
Instead, she was a new trainee
And made a lot of cups of tea
For more important policemen who,
It seemed, had better things to do –
Especially one Sergeant Jude,
A horrid little man, most rude.
He called Rose up by phone and sneered,
"A dog detective – that's just weird.
I think you should be chasing sticks
And doing other doggy tricks.
But since you're here, you pay your way
And go and get my lunch today.

WANTED

I want some toast with hot baked beans,
Then biscuits and some tangerines."
So Rose peered meekly round his door
And left his order on the floor.
She fortunately did not meet
This man who spoke with such conceit,
As he was in the toilet so
She dashed out quick as billy-o.
In private, though, she shed a tear;
It wasn't fair this man should jeer.
But then she thought, "I'll show this berk
Just how hard dog detectives work!"

The next day, Rose was summoned to
The room of Chief Inspector Drew,
A most important policeman who's
Quite often on the TV news.
His nickname is Inspector Ace –
He's never failed to solve a case!

And Rose felt very much in awe,
As she knocked shyly on his door.
"Come in," he cried, "please take a seat."
He waved her to a leather suite.
"Now, Rose," a frown took up his face,
"This is a most important case.
A scoundrel, as I'm sure you've seen,
Has robbed her Majesty the Queen!
He took her crowns, her pearls, her rings,
Her clothes and other cherished things.
He even took," he growled beneath
His breath, "her Majesty's false teeth!
And so we have to track him down.
The Queen is in her dressing gown
And can't be seen in public while
She has a dreadful toothless smile!"

"I understand, Inspector Drew,"
Rose gasped, "What *are* we going to do?"
This nice man answered quietly.
"Well now Rose, you see it was me
Who asked that it were you they sent.
I know your powers with a scent.
We have a great clue as a starter –
This man is a dreadful farter!
He made rude noises as he crept
Around whilst all the Palace slept,
Until one fart was oh-so-loud –
It sounded like a thundercloud!
The Queen woke up and shrieked in fright,
And off he ran - around midnight.
The palace, even now, is tainted.
Such is the smell, some staff have fainted!
So I want you to find this stinker
And bring him down hook, line and sinker!"

* * *

The next day, Rose was at the scene,
Exactly where the thief had been.
She saw the window that he'd smashed,
The footprints showing how he'd dashed
Across the hall to parachute
Away with all the royal loot.

DO NOT CROSS
DO NOT CROSS
DO NOT CROSS
DO NOT CROSS
DO NOT CROSS
DO NOT CROSS
3
9
12

And goodness gracious, it was smelly –
This man had problems with his belly!
Rose took a moment to record
The odour to her memory board
With other memorabilia –
It smelt a tad familiar?
Then down the Palace steps she went
To follow the repulsive scent.
Rose raced off through the nearby park,
With one determined little bark.
She sniffed at grown-ups on their phones
And children eating ice cream cones.
She passed a soldier on his watch
And poked her nose up near his crotch!
It gave the man an awful fright,
But no, he didn't smell quite right.
She nosed at people on their backs
And foreign tourists in their packs.

As one poor Dutchman, please don't laugh,
Bent down to take a photograph,
Rose dipped her nose inside his pants –
It tickled like a swarm of ants,
Which made him give a sudden shake
And drop his camera in the lake!
He swung round with a filthy glare,
But Rose ran on – no time to care.
She hurtled through a winding street,
Still faster did her brave heart beat.
Rose knew that she was getting near,
Excitement conquered any fear!
The scent led to a quiet road
With one lone house, and Rose tiptoed
To scan the curtains, tightly drawn,
And bags of rubbish on the lawn.

Rose settled down and lay in wait
Outside a rusty garden gate.
She sat an hour, maybe more.
The door swung open and she saw
A young man in his dressing gown.
(Rose ducked and kept her head well down.)
He carried out a pile of tins
And walked towards the garden bins;
All baked beans cans and giant-sized.
Rose startled as she realised –
A windy stomach – what that means
Is that the thief must like baked beans!
That smell Rose knew she'd smelt before!
She charged the robber to the floor,
And with her paws, this gentle hound
Did pin him face-down on the ground.
Rose nosed his ankles open wide –
The man was truly horrified.
"You filthy beast," he yelled, "decease!
I order you, I'm in the police!
You let me go, I do not jest,
You're under serious arrest!"
Rose sniffed his bottom with delight –
She knew that she had got it right,
As, to her rather great relief,
The scent exactly matched the thief.
This stinky man, now semi-nude,
Rose knew that it was Sergeant Jude!

So Sergeant Jude was put in cuffs
And led away with angry huffs.
The Queen's possessions were retrieved
And everyone was most relieved
That she could smile and not be teased.
Inspector Drew was super-pleased!
"Well done, young Rose," he said with pride,
"From now on, you work by my side.
I never did trust Sergeant Jude –
He had a nasty attitude.
But we will make a winning team!"
Rose couldn't stop her happy beam.

All this has brought her great acclaim –
They've even made our Rose a dame.
She goes round in a limousine!
She's got a medal from the Queen!
And meanwhile, Sergeant Jude is well,
Though locked up in a prison cell.
(He has to stay in quarantine
If he eats even one baked bean!)
He spends his daytimes chopping sticks
And doing other boring tricks,
And he should never, now he knows,
Have under-estimated Rose!

The Doctor

Keith Gray lives with his mum and dad
And sister, Claire. He's not that bad.
He talks politely, doesn't yell,
He always does his homework well.
He doesn't ever skive off school
Or punch his friends or play the fool.
His room is tidy, nice and clean.
His hair is brushed and nails pristine.
There's just one tricky thing with Keith:
At meals he sits with gritted teeth,
And not one vegetable or fruit
Will ever make it down the chute!
"BIG YUCK!" he cries in pure disgust,
If green things lurk beneath a crust.
Boiled sprouts and cabbage meet with hate,
He leaves them firmly on his plate.
And if his mummy tries to hide
Some peas or broccoli inside
His chicken pie, our Keith will bawl
And fling them at the kitchen wall!
Through practice he is also able
To slip his food beneath the table
And hide it quickly out of sight,
Disposing of it late at night.

His sister found one day, like glue,
Bananas clogging up the loo!
(It took his father's welly boot
To free the rotting mass of fruit!)
His mum found sandwiches inside
Keith's sock drawer, where he'd tried to hide
Them for the truly awful sin
Of having bits of lettuce in!
Keith's mummy tried 'most every ploy
To get nutrition down her boy.

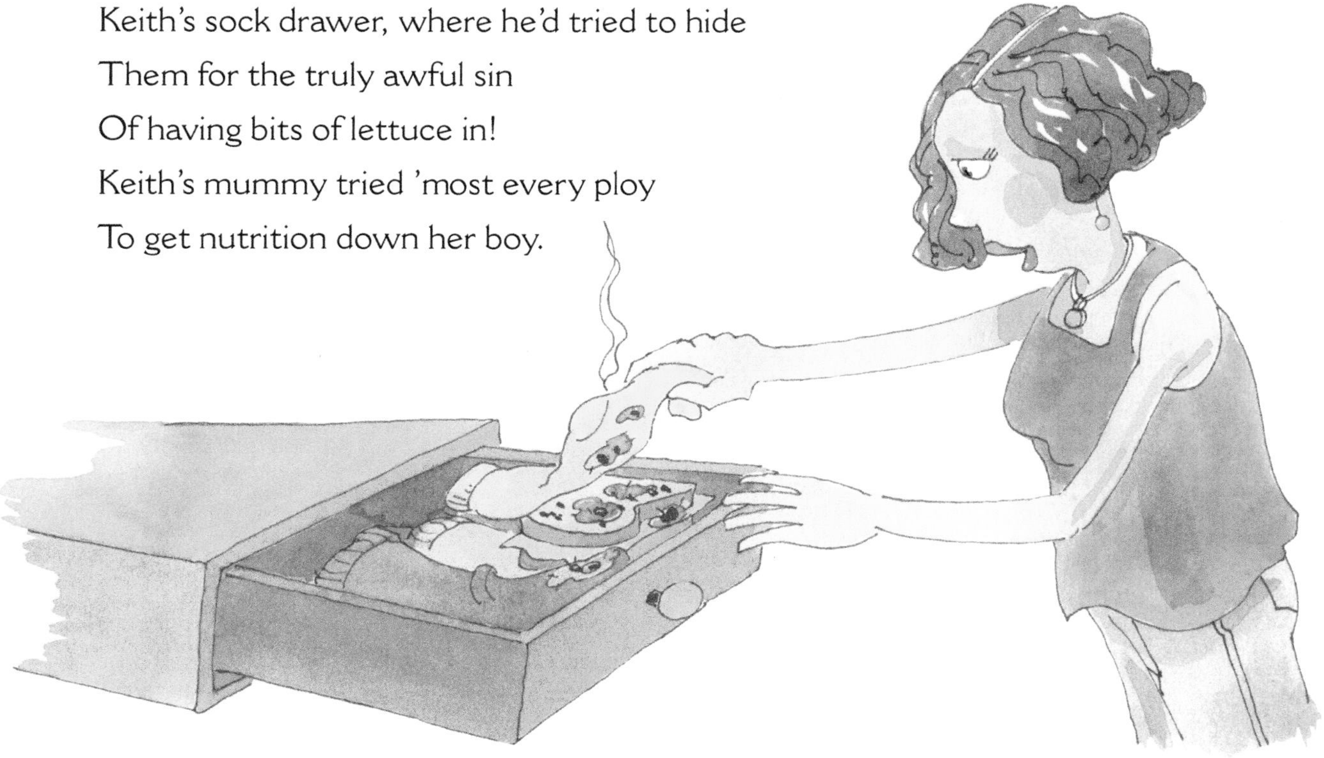

She cooked things nicely, added honey,
Promised extra pocket money,
But Keith gave back sustained rebuff
And one day Mummy'd had enough.
She crossly grabbed the telephone
And in a most determined tone
Demanded, with a fearsome scowl,
For Keith to see their doctor, Owl.

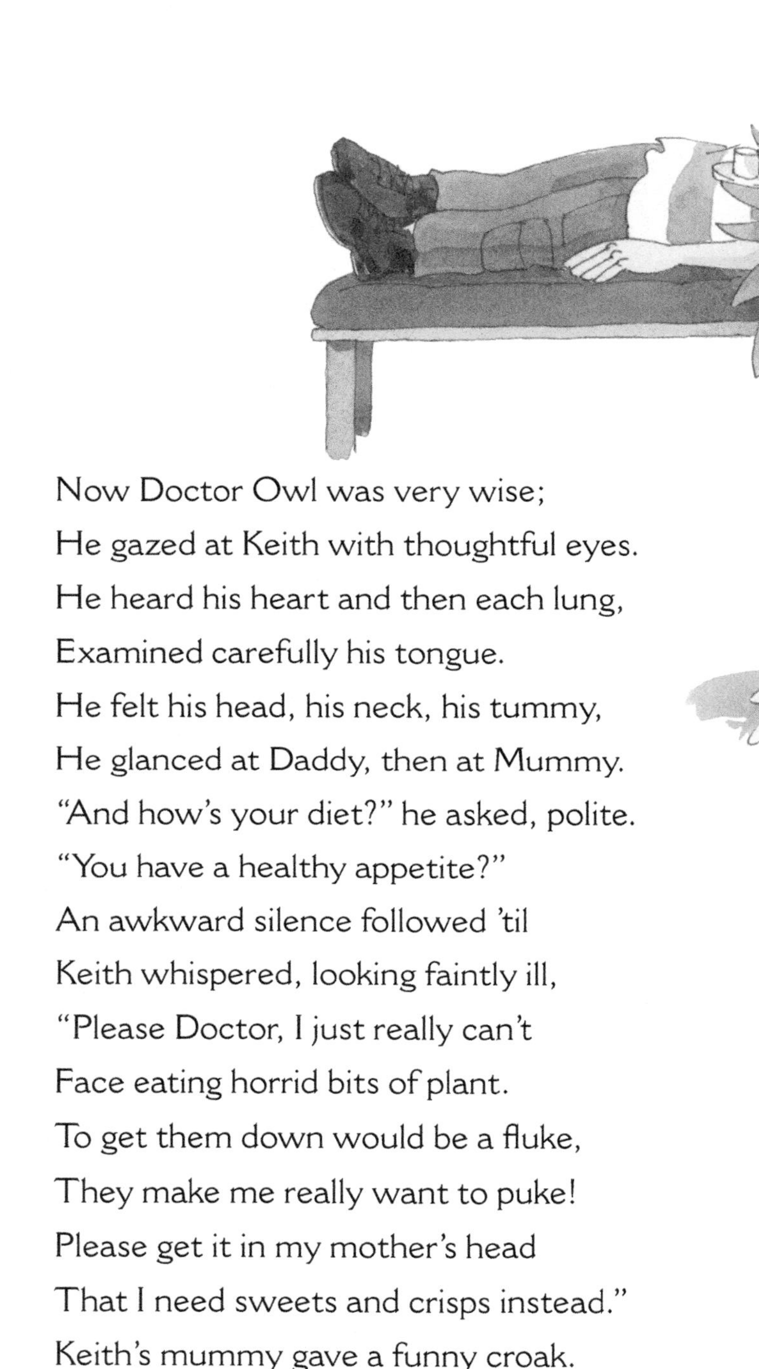

Now Doctor Owl was very wise;
He gazed at Keith with thoughtful eyes.
He heard his heart and then each lung,
Examined carefully his tongue.
He felt his head, his neck, his tummy,
He glanced at Daddy, then at Mummy.
"And how's your diet?" he asked, polite.
"You have a healthy appetite?"
An awkward silence followed 'til
Keith whispered, looking faintly ill,
"Please Doctor, I just really can't
Face eating horrid bits of plant.
To get them down would be a fluke,
They make me really want to puke!
Please get it in my mother's head
That I need sweets and crisps instead."
Keith's mummy gave a funny croak.
Keith thought she might go up in smoke!
Her mouth snapped like an alligator
And Keith knew he was for it later!

The doctor gazed out from beneath
His fluffy brows and stared at Keith.
For quite some time, he didn't blink,
Then gave Keith's mum a tiny wink.

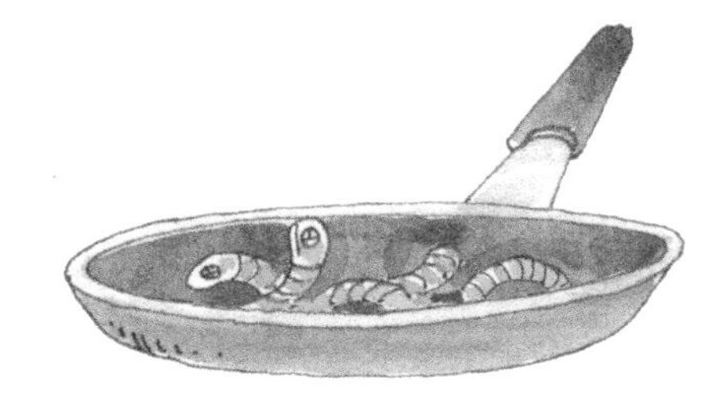

"I think I see," said Doctor Owl,
"It seems you have a fussy bowel,
So when you try to eat your greens,
It sends them back and hence that means
You may require a different diet."
The doctor paused and all was quiet.

"So what I'm minded to suggest
Is that you give the veg a rest,
And then, instead, incorporate
Some tasty protein on your plate.
Myself, I like young rats and lizards
With spiders, grubs or chicken gizzards.
Then earthworms too – don't overlook
Them for they're very quick to cook!
You simply bring them to the boil
Or fry them up in olive oil!"

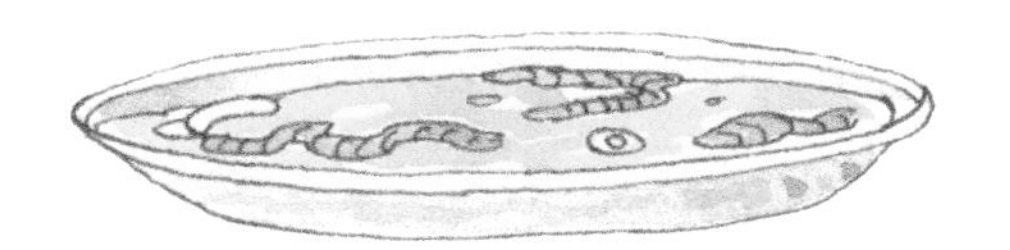

Keith sat in disbelieving quiet:
This sounded a horrendous diet!
But Doctor Owl had closed his file.
He waved them out, with knowing smile.

* * *

And so that evening, for his tea,
Keith didn't get a single pea.
Instead, he had some boiled up mice
With spiders' legs – it wasn't nice.
The next day, it was jellyfish
With frogs' spawn. Keith began to wish
They'd never been to Doctor Owl.
His mealtimes now were truly foul!
His sister munched through parsnip bake
Or sausage mash then apple cake,
And laughed at Keith's disgusting fare.
Keith muttered, "Oh just shut up, Claire."
But privately, he came to mourn
The loss of carrots, leeks and corn!

Then, on the twenty-first of May,
There came a very special day.
Keith's sister, Claire, was turning eight
And so, of course, to celebrate,
Their mum prepared a lovely meal,
Whilst Keith sat down to tripe and eel!
Then Claire was given cherry pie
And Keith let out a heartfelt cry.

"OK, OK! I've had enough!
I can't eat this revolting stuff!
Please give me back BOY FOOD. I vow
I'll eat the vegetation now!"
His parents beamed with great relief,
Whilst Claire looked on in disbelief.
But Keith forever kept his word;
No matter what, they never heard
Complaints that fruit and veg were hateful.
He ate them up, and, boy, was grateful!

Now some years later, you might find
A restaurant of a special kind.
They serve all kinds of lovely food,
Some baked, some boiled, some fried, some stewed.
It has a chef who's world-renowned –
Yes, *Sir* Keith Gray can now be found
Creating gourmet food with pride,
From different cultures far and wide –
Like Greek, Chinese, Hungarian –
And all is vegetarian!
So what's it called, this famous place?
A smile will spread across your face.
You'll see the photo, cheek by jowl,
Of Sir Keith with 'The Crafty Owl'.

THE LIFEGUARD

I bet you think this tale's a bore.
You've known it word for word since four.
The sweet princess, it makes you wince,
And how the frog became a prince.
The magic spell, the golden ball,
I know, I know, you've heard it all.
You heard it lying in your cot,
Perhaps you read it on the pot!
And though it's hard, I beg you, please,
Abandon all these memories,
And as with every pantomime,
We'll start with "Once upon a time,
There was a rather ugly girl,
The daughter of a wealthy earl,
And on the day she heard her fate,
The girl began to meditate.
"Now Dad," she said, "let's get it straight –
I'll bring that story up to date,
And people will begin to see,
They'll make no fairy tale of me!"
To start off with the overhaul,
She threw away her golden ball.

Instead, she was a Star Wars fan
And bought the latest Action Man.
She guzzled beer, which made her drunk.
She had her hair done like a punk.
She didn't have a single friend
And drove her parents round the bend.
The day she dyed the budgie black,
Her mother had a heart attack!
"My darling Bess," her father sighed,
"You'll never make a proper bride."
The poor earl rolled his eyes and said,
"I wish you'd marry Ethelred –
A charming man," he voiced with pride.
"A horrid creep," the girl replied.

Then one day in the month July,
Bess took her kitten, Sweetie-pie,
And clambered up the garden tree,
But then, a tad unfortunately,
She gave the cat a little shove
Towards a higher branch above
And Sweetie slipped. She flew beyond
The wall and into next door's pond!
Bess peered at her with great dismay
And jumped the wall without delay.
She searched the pond and quickly found
The kitten, who had nearly drowned,
And as young Bess could plainly see,
Was sinking rather rapidly.
Poor Sweetie's fate looked very grim
As Bess did not know how to swim.
So as in every fairy tale,
The helpless girl let out a wail,
And then, of course, (it's what you feared)
A rather cocky frog appeared.
"Stand back," he cried, "and do not fear –
Amazing Super-Frog is here!"
Bess looked at him with widened eyes;
Perhaps this was a good surprise.
Then something clicked, she said, "Not you..."
The fairy tale was coming true!

The frog awaited no reply.
Instead, he gave a mighty cry.
As Bess shrieked, "Oh my saints alive!"
He did a perfect forward dive.
Frog shouted, "Kitty, here I am,"
And quickly to the cat he swam.
He grabbed her with a strong green hand
And bought her safely back to land.

Frog gave our Bess a winning smile.
He said, "I think I've passed my trial.
Now kiss me, darling, on my face
And everything falls into place!"
Bess looked at Frog's revolting skin
And gulped as something deep within
Did threaten to regurgitate
The food she'd had on lunchtime's plate.
"I can't," she said, "I'd rather eat
My dinner from a toilet seat
Than have to kiss your slimy zits.
I'm sorry, can we call it quits?"
Frog looked at her, annoyed, and said,
"You stupid girl, have you not read
The book? Do you not comprehend
How all this is supposed to end?"

"I'm sorry, Frog," Bess stood her ground.
"I'm super grateful that you found
My Sweetie-pie and saved the day,
But could I pay another way?"
"OK," snapped Frog and glared, "As such,
I do not really charge that much.
I ask for only one small fee;
A few things you must do for me.
But if you ever break your bond
I'll throw your cat back in the pond.
So here it is," the sly Frog said,
"To me you must donate your bed,
Your pretty frocks, your fireside chair,
And show me how to grow my hair!
Your necklaces, your rocking horse,
Your pocket money too, of course.
This goes on 'til you're twenty three,
Which seems quite reasonable to me."

The future didn't sound too bright,
But Bess took Frog back for the night,
And Sweetie, who was well and calm,
Sat safely under Bess's arm.
That night, Bess lay upon the floor
And tried to block the thunderous snore
From Frog, who meanwhile laid his head
On Bess's gorgeous feather bed!
But then, at twenty-five to four,
Bess screamed, "I can't take any more!
The deal is off, I can't agree."
(She locked Frog in the lavatory!)
As soon as Bess had turned away,
She heard the froggy's weak voice say,
"Oh Bess, you'll see no more of me,
If you will only set me free."
More quietly, he made the vow,
"Well, not through eyes that you have now."
And thus, he managed to deceive
Our Bess, who was a touch naïve.
She stepped across the bedroom floor
And, kindly, she unlocked the door.
Frog sprang straight out and cried, "Well, well!
So now it's time to cast MY spell!"
He laughed, "And as for you, my pet,
This foolishness you'll soon regret.

You see, if you had just agreed
To kiss me as the rules decreed,
All would be well and now you'd see
Me as a prince, your groom-to-be!
But as you broke the rules instead,
You'll never be a newly-wed.
In fact, as you're about to learn,
Your life will take a different turn!"
He waved his arms and cried a chant,
"Batrachia Bessa, now supplant."
Bess stared at him, her mouth agog,
And in a flash became a frog!

The Hairdresser

The hairdresser's at Number 10
Is known to all as 'Lion's Den.'
Its owner is a lion called Ray.
He's open every single day.
He's friendly and extremely kind,
Although he's deaf and partly blind
(For shortly after Ray was born,
He tangled with a rhino horn!)
He greets you with a beaming smile,
He's expert at 'most any style.
No matter if they're dark or fair,
Ray just loves cutting children's hair.
He rubs your head with gentle paws
And combs your hair with careful claws.
You get a massive lollipop
To suck before you get the chop.
With boys, around the floor Ray glides
And whistles up short back and sides.
His scissors give a final flick
And leave you looking very slick.
It's different though for little girls.
He works hard for those tumbling curls
And ringlets, plaits and ponytails –
No matter what, he never fails

To beautify their glossy tresses
And make them feel like real princesses.
So parents gather in their flocks
For Ray to tend their children's locks.

Another thing you should be told,
Dear Ray is getting fairly old,
And as he always gives his best,
Come end of day he needs his rest.
He labours hard from eight 'til five
And sometimes barely feels alive
Come closing time at four, when he's
Quite frankly nearly on his knees.

* * *

One Friday, after half past four,
While Ray was sweeping up the floor
And thinking what he'd have for tea,
The doorbell rang impatiently.
It took a while for Ray to hear
Because of his defective ear.
But then there came a mighty crack.
Ray nearly had a heart attack!
As someone rapped the window pane
With what looked like a twisted cane,
Clutched tightly by a warty crone.
There came a nasty, whining tone.
"Why, you in there, you dimblewit,
This door is shut! Come open it!"
Ray did his best to stay composed.
"I'm sorry, Ma'am, but I am closed."

"No good!" she shrieked with urgency.
"This is a hair emergency.
My sweet son here on Saturday
Is in a most important play.
He plays the lead, our little hero,
The starring role, the Emperor Nero."
(To Ray this was a mystery –
He'd never studied history,
And least of all the Roman kind
When emperors weren't sound of mind.)
"So let us in," she bawled again.
"I'll give you to the count of ten."

Snarling like an injured leopard,
"No-one disobeys Jean Shepherd."
Ray sighed and trundled to the door.
This wasn't what he'd bargained for,
But as the only shop in town,
He felt he couldn't let them down.
He opened up and was appalled.
Ms Shepherd was completely bald!
She had a nasty pointy nose
With weeping blisters, three of those.
Ray felt his stomach cramping quick.
He really thought he might be sick.
He turned to greet the little lad
And saw that he was just as bad.
His hair was long and face was mean,
But worst of all, his skin was green!
The boy spoke up, "My name is Wayne."
He looked at Ray with great disdain.
"I need to look, you silly cat,
Like Hugh," declared the little brat.
"As well as being my best buddy,
He's acting as the understudy."
Now bear in mind that Ray was tired
And so his ears weren't fully fired.
So when Wayne said, "to look like Hugh",
Poor Ray just heard, "to look like YOU".

"To look like me?" His mind felt tense.
It didn't seem to make much sense.
No time to think – a sharpened talon
Pushed him back inside the salon.
So as the outside light grew dim,
Ray worked to make Wayne look like him.

It was his greatest challenge yet.
No matter what, he couldn't get
Wayne's hair to stand on end - in vain,
He tried to tease a fluffy mane.
(The young star meanwhile had a stab
At peeling off a massive scab,
Whilst Mrs Shepherd seemed most keen
On 'Bald and Lovely' magazine.)
Ray combed, he twirled, he gave his all,
But Wayne's lank hair would only fall.
Eventually, with great dismay,
He had to use a can of spray
And then a tin of copper paint.
(The foul smell nearly made him faint!)
He carefully unwrapped the foils
And stood back to review his toils.
Although he still felt very stressed,
Ray had to say he was impressed.
He thanked his lucky stars, Orion.
Wayne looked just like a little lion!

“I think we’re done,” Ray said and he
Held up the mirror cautiously.
“And now, you will appreciate,
It’s really getting rather late.
So best of luck in your school play.
Ma’am, would you come this way to pay?”
There came the most appalling noise,
As Wayne abandoned all his poise

"What *have* you done?" he screamed aloud.
"I look just like a fluffy cloud,
A dandelion, a daffodil.
You'll pay for this – oh yes, you will!"
His mother quickly took his place,
A look of venom on her face.
"You stupid creature, where's your brain?
What have you done to darling Wayne?"
An evil glint a'crossed her eye,
She drew a hairpin way up high
And with a terrifying roar,
She stuck it in the lion's paw!
Ray's world went white as tapioca –
The pin felt like a red hot poker.
He shot up with a frantic shout
And wildly tried to pull it out.
He flung his paws and punched the air,
Whilst hair things scattered everywhere.
The Shepherds cackled with a sneer,
But they were just a tad too near.
He never meant to do them wrong,
But Ray was panicking and strong.
He caught the Shepherds with a blow
And saw them down like skittles go.
They bashed and splatted, head on head,
And whacked the floor, where both lay dead!

The awful sight made poor Ray quake.
He knew he'd made a huge mistake.
He uttered out a little wail,
"Oh please don't let me go to jail.
My Lord, I swear, I never meant
To harm – it was an accident."
And for a while he rocked in fear,
Until he had a great idea!
And so you'll see, when next you pop
To get your hair cut at Ray's shop,
A lovely pair of model heads
Look out across the flowerbeds.
The heads give you a sneaky peek
At Ray's new hairstyles of the week,
And hungry folk might like to buy
A tasty, fresh, hot "Shepherd's pie"!

Carolyn May was born in Chertsey in the UK and grew up in Guildford. She went on to study Experimental Psychology at Oxford University and now works for part of the UK's National Health Service. Carolyn has always loved writing humorous rhyming stories about animals for children, and wrote the first version of *The Lifeguard* when she was 13 herself. Many years later, she was inspired whilst on holiday in Cyprus to write a story about a horse who wanted to be a famous football referee and the other characters came along quickly afterwards! Carolyn is already working on her next book about another troublesome group of animals..!

Laura Liberatore was born in Caracas, Venezuela. During her childhood and at school she always loved drawing and realised early on that she wanted to become an Illustrator and graphic designer. She went on to graduate from the Instituto de Diseño Fundación Neumann in Caracas, specialising in hand drawings and computer design.
Since that point Laura has illustrated over 20 children's books and has won numerous awards for her work. She is still happier than ever to be illustrating new children's books, especially stories featuring animals!

All characters and events appearing in this work are fictitious. Any similarity to actual persons or animals, living or dead, is purely coincidental.

Lightning Source UK Ltd.
Milton Keynes UK
UKOW07f1357121216
289793UK00006B/53/P